Copyright © 2012 by NordSüd Verlag AG, Heinrichstrasse 249,
CH-8005 Zürich, Switzerland.
First published in Switzerland under the title *Gans anders*.
English text copyright © 2012 by North-South Books Inc., 300 East 42nd Street,
New York 10017.

First published in the United States, Great Britain, Canada, Australia, and New
Zealand in 2012 by North-South Books, Inc., an imprint of NordSüd Verlag AG,
CH-8005 Zürich, Switzerland.

Translated by David Henry Wilson.
Distributed in the United States by North-South Books Inc., New York 10017.
Library of Congress Cataloging-in-Publication Data is available.
ISBN: 978-0-7358-4076-8 (trade edition)
1 3 5 7 9 • 10 8 6 4 2
Printed in China by Hung Hing Off-set printing Co., Ltd. Manufactured in
Shenzhen, Guangdong, October 2011
www.northsouth.com

Sebastian Loth

# Zelda the Varigoose

NorthSouth
New York / London

# GOOSNAIL
It doesn't matter where I roam,
Because I always feel at home.

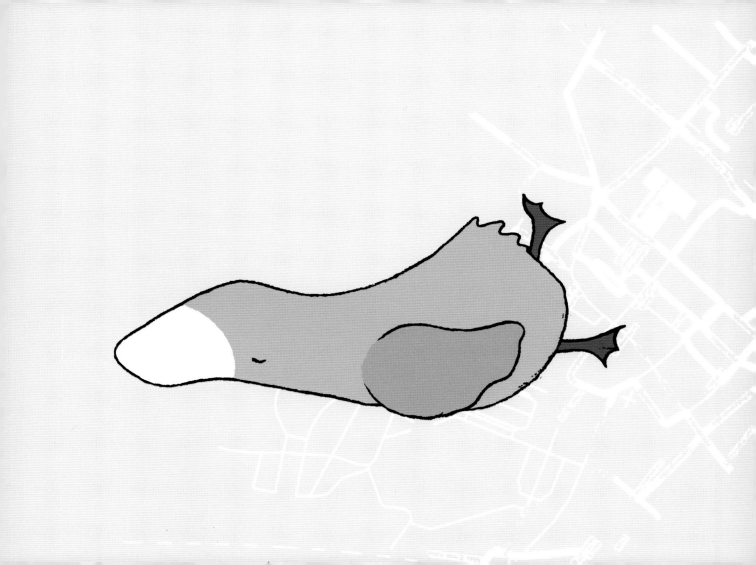

# GOOSEPHANT

If I caught cold, then I suppose
I'd need an hour to blow my nose.

# GOOSEY BEE

Life in a beehive's very sweet,
As there's lots of honey for me to eat.

# CHAMELEGOOSE

I may be there, but you won't know—
I change my color wherever I go.

# GOOGIRAFFE

I can look over the top of the tree,
So I see you. Can you see me?

# GOOSEY GLOWWORM

I'm not afraid to go out at night,
As wherever I am, I shine so bright.

# GOOSQUID

I can squirt out clouds of ink.
Good to hide in—not to drink!

# GOOSEY PEACOCK

In all the world you'll never see
A prouder, lovelier bird than me.

# LADYBUG GOOSE

Don't chase me away whatever you do.
I'll bring you luck if I land on you.

# WHALEGOOSE
There is no animal bigger than me,
But I can swim like a fish in the sea.

# BUTTERFLOOSE
Gracefully *I* spend hours and hours
Fluttering all around the flowers.

Sometimes as I swim, crawl, fly,
I ask myself, "Just who am I?"
The answer's plain: a goose—that's me,
And that's what I most like to be.

for Dagmar

My thanks to:
Daniela for her support—Bernd and Birte for the brainstorming—Andrea for
her cooperation—Theo for the clover—Barbara for the honeycomb—Silke
for the peacock feathers—Claudia for the subjunctive—and Dagmar for the
inspiration without which this book would never have existed! And also to
everyone who helped to choose the pictures.